Once upon a time there was a
hungry family with seven children. One day, their mother
mixed up a wonderfully sweet
pancake batter from sugar,
milk, yeast, eggs, butter and
flour. After the batter rose, she
poured it into the frying pan. A
delicious aroma filled the air as
the pancake cooked.

"Oh, Mommy," the seven children whined at the same time, "when are we going to get some of that pancake?"

"As soon as it's cooked, when the crust is crisp and golden," she replied.

But the pancake saw all those gaping, hungry mouths, and all those greedy eyes watching him. He was frightened. He didn't want to be eaten! With a great leap, he jumped out of the frying pan knocking it to the ground, rolled across the floor, out the door, and down the street.

"Where do you think you're going?" the shocked mother shouted. She grabbed the frying pan and the spoon and ran after the pancake. But she was very fat and couldn't run fast enough. She tried to stop the pancake by throwing dishes and cups at him, but to no avail. Her husband and children joined the chase.

"Stop that pancake!" they

yelled as they ran after him. "Grab it!" they begged.

But the pancake was so fast on his feet that he soon left the hungry family far behind. They saw him disappear around the corner of a house. At that time, they finally gave up the chase and settled for a dinner of dry bread.

"Hi, there, old man," said the pancake.

"Don't run away so fast. Stay and let me nibble at your middle. I've always loved pancakes."

"No way!" the pancake stammered. "I just escaped from a big, hungry family. What makes you think I'm going to let *you* eat me?"

Meanwhile, out in the street, the pancake had almost run into an old man.

"Good morning, pancake," the old man said.

With that, he sped away. But it wasn't long before he met a big rooster.

"Good morning, pancake," crowed the rooster.

"Hi, there, rooster," the pancake said nervously.

"What's your hurry?" asked the rooster. "Rest here awhile and let me eat a little bit of you. The farmer's wife forgot to give me my corn this morning."

"I just escaped from a big, hungry family and an old man," the pancake answered, "and I'm certainly not going to stay here and let you eat me instead of a handful of corn!"

He took off at top speed, thumbing his nose at the rooster as he ran. He ran and

ran until he came upon a big, fat hen with gleaming feathers, perched on a fence.

"Hello, pancake," clucked the hen.

"Hello," the pancake nodded.

"What's with all this running? Stick around and let me peck at your crispy edges. I overslept today and my friends ate everything in sight. I'm so hungry!"

"I already escaped from a big, hungry family, an old man, and a rooster. I'm not going to stop now and let myself be eaten by you!"

"Come on, pancake, just a little peck!" she begged.

The pancake didn't pay any attention. He rolled away as fast as he could, muttering to himself. Everyone he met wanted to eat him because he was so crisp and golden and smelled so good.

All his running made him tired, so when he came upon a wading pool he stopped to rest for awhile. Just as he got settled, a duck waddled by.

"Good morning, pancake," quacked the duck.

"Oh, hello."

"Did you stop here to let me eat you? How nice!" the duck said with a smile.

"Wait a minute!" snorted the pancake. "So far I've escaped from a big, hungry family, an old man, a rooster, and a big, fat hen. You don't stand a chance."

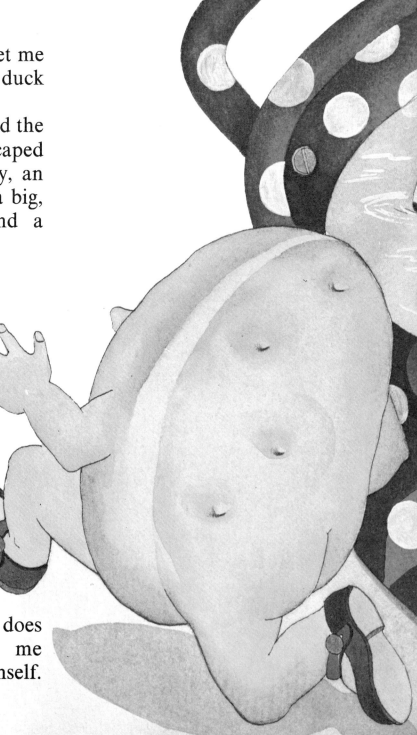

He hurried away. "Why does everyone want to eat me today?" he asked himself.

"What's a poor little crispy golden pancake who smells so good have to do to get a little peace and quiet?"

He was still mumbling when he noticed a goose blocking his path. It seemed very big and threatening with its yellow beak and shiny feathers.

"Well, good morning, pancake," honked the goose.

"Not again!" sighed the pancake.

"Why are you going away so fast? Stop a moment and catch your breath so I can have a good snap at you. I haven't found any frogs or berries in the marshes today, and I'm in need of a good meal. So are my babies over there in the little hut. Do you see them? They're waiting for their dinner, and you would fit the order so nicely!"

"Oh, no, I wouldn't!" screamed the pancake. "I've just escaped from a big, hungry family, an old man, a rooster, a big, fat hen, *and* a duck. You think I'm going to let *you* eat me? You're wasting your breath, mother goose."

He ran away so quickly that he looked like a ball instead of a pancake. He hoped his troubles were over for the day, but, alas, no such luck. Standing right in front of him, looking him right in the eye, was an enormous gander.

"Good morning, pancake," bellowed the gander.

"Don't tell me."

"What's your hurry? Come into my house and rest so I can eat you. It's dinner time, you know."

"Not for you!" cried the pancake. "I have escaped from a big, hungry family, an old man, a rooster, a big, fat hen, a duck, and a goose. I'm not going to let *anyone* eat me, thank you very much!"

The gander ran after him but wasn't fast enough. Fear for his life gave the pancake added speed! He ran and ran, oh, how that pancake ran!

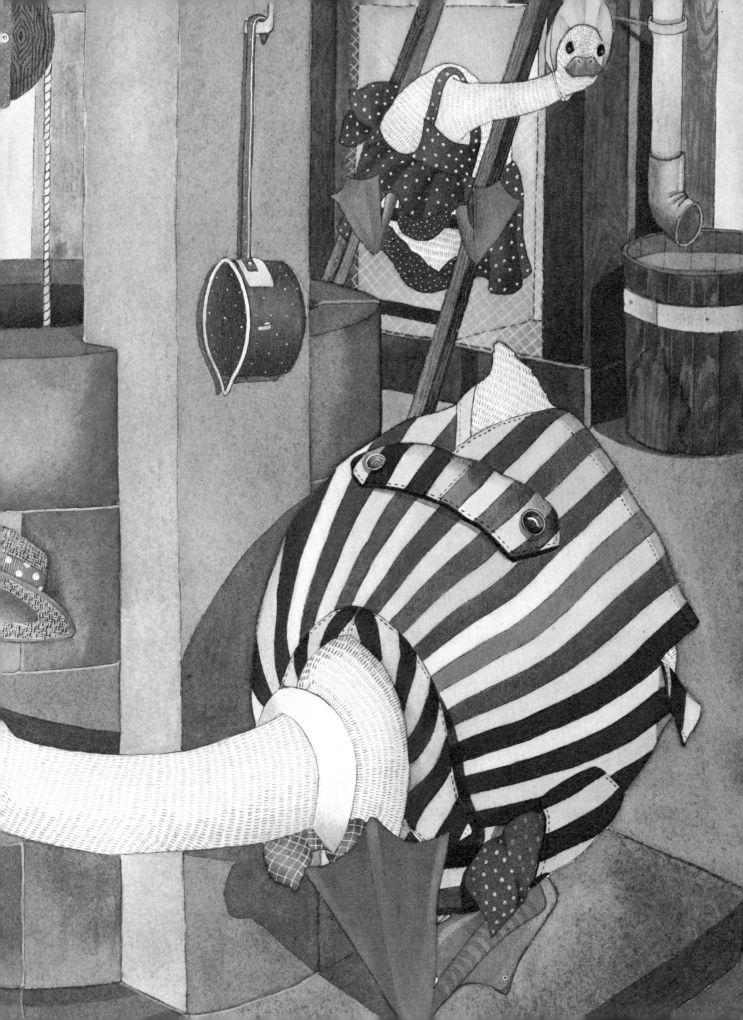

But he wasn't looking where he was headed, and he bumped into a round pink pig who was dozing in the cool mud during the mid-day sun.

"Good morning, pancake," oinked the pig, opening one eye.

"No! You can't eat me!" the pancake shouted, without even slowing down.

"Who said I wanted to eat you?" The pig stretched and yawned. "I don't even like pancakes," he said.

When the pancake heard that, he stopped running and looked at the pig gratefully.

"How about going for a walk?" suggested the pig.

The pancake was tired of running. It seemed like a good idea, so off they went. They strolled leisurely until they came to a river.

"Let's cross and walk on the other side where it's nice and shady," urged the pig.

"I can't," sighed the pancake. "If I get wet, I'll sink."

"You're right," the pig agreed. "But if you jump on my back, I'll carry you over."

"That's very nice of you," the pancake acknowledged. "But I don't want to be a bother."

"Don't worry about it," the pig smiled reassuringly. "The pleasure's all mine."

The pancake jumped on the pig's back and they went in the water. Suddenly, the pig turned around, opened his mouth wide, and gobbled up the pancake.

And that's the end of the story, because that was the end of the pancake.

This is the end of the story.
Now close the book,
turn it upside down,
and you can begin
another tale.

never returned. The widow tried vainly to keep her daughter quiet, but Rose just could not stop complaining. Finally, her mother had enough, and threw Rose out of the house.

Rose went to the village to beg for shelter, but one word from her mouth and the doors slammed in her face. She did the only thing she could. She went into the woods she hated, built a crude hut, and lived on grass and berries. Her temper never improved. She was the same bitter, selfish, envious woman who had only bad wishes for everyone. She muttered to herself in discontent and anger. Even the forest animals avoided her.

One very dark evening, she left her miserable hut, which was filled with snakes and toads, to go for a walk. Unable to see the edge of a cliff, she slipped and fell. She was killed instantly on the rocks far below.

This is the end of the story.
Now close the book,
turn it upside down,
and you can begin another tale.

Whatever objections he might have had about his son marrying a commoner vanished after he spoke with her for a while. At her feet, the floor glittered with jewels larger and more perfect than any that had ever been seen before. The flowers—roses, jasmine, violets, pansies—perfumed the air.

The king approved the marriage which took place just one week later. The wedding was the finest celebration the kingdom had ever seen. The fountains flowed with wine instead of water, the cooks made pastries and cakes for everyone, and the streets overflowed with flowers. From that day forward, the young couple lived in happiness.

But what about Rose? And the widow? What ever happened to them?

They had nothing to match Hyacinth's happiness. Whenever Rose spoke masses of snakes and toads jumped out, in all shapes and sizes. Eventually the house was so full of them that the two wretches didn't know where to put their feet. The farmyard animals

word. Her story moved him, but her beauty and gentleness fascinated him. He thought that this beautiful, weeping young woman was just the sort of wife he had been wanting. Not only was she wonderful, generous, kind and lovely, but she had an inexhaustible dowry.

"I've never met anyone like you, Hyacinth," he said. He had fallen in love with her and asked her to be his wife.

Hyacinth accepted immediately. He helped her onto his horse and together they rode to his father's spectacular royal palace.

The prince had made a wise choice. As soon as the king saw Hyacinth, he was conquered by her beauty and goodness.

young prince on horseback happened by on his way home from a hunt. He heard Hyacinth's sobs and pulled his horse to a stop. He looked around and saw a lovely young woman crying as though her heart would break.

"Why are you crying," the prince asked. "What happened?"

Hyacinth looked up and dried her eyes. The prince saw how beautiful they were despite her tears.

Hyacinth explained and with every word she spoke, gardenias, pearls, sapphires fell from her lips. When she finished her long story a fortune had collected on the grass at her feet.

The prince heard her every

The widow didn't listen. She kept after Hyacinth, hitting her with the stick whenever she could get near. Hyacinth had to get away. She ran to the forest, leaving the home she had lived in all her life. Her mother called after her, "Don't dare come back."

Hyacinth sat under a tree, gasping for breath, weeping over her bad luck. A handsome

three snakes slithered out of her mouth. Her mother shrieked so loudly that all the farmyard animals ran away.

"What is this," she cried. "It must be your sister's fault! I know it. Just wait until I get my hands on her!"

The widow grabbed a heavy stick and searched for Hyacinth to beat her. Hyacinth fled in terror. She tried to explain that it wasn't her fault, that something strange must have happened for her sister to have been so unlucky.

She had never wanted to come to this dark, lonely place to begin with. She only came to please her mother. She finally got tired of waiting and went home dragging the empty bottle which she hadn't even bothered to fill. Her mother was eagerly waiting for her. "Well, what happened?"

Rose shrugged her shoulders. "I didn't see anyone," she said, and as she spoke two toads and

you can think again!" Rose answered. "If you're so thirsty, use your hands."

"You're not very polite, are you?" replied the fairy. "I'm going to teach you a lesson about bad manners that will show you what you get for such selfish behavior."

"Oh, yes? What could *you* do?" she laughed at the fairy's threat.

"From now on, whenever you speak, toads and snakes will jump out of your mouth."

Rose folded her arms across her chest and scowled defiantly. She wasn't concerned since she was sure that the woman with such power was a ragged old hag, not a lady in fine clothes.

Rose waited and waited, growing more and more tired, and more and more impatient.

Rose immediately complained to her mother, "Who, me? Go to the spring like a servant? Never!"

But her mother insisted, and convinced her to go. Rose put on her fanciest dress and took a dainty glass bottle instead of the heavy jug. She grumbled to herself all the way through the woods.

When she reached the spring she didn't see anyone nearby and became even more annoyed. She was afraid to be alone in the dark, scary woods. A lady appeared after a while, dressed in an elegant gown with jewelry to suit her finery. It was the same fairy who had come to Hyacinth as an old woman. This time she wanted to test Rose and see just how bad her manners really were.

"Would you be so kind as to offer me a little water, my dear child?" she asked.

"If you think I came all this way to get *you* a drink of water,

ing?" she asked Hyacinth. "Flowers and jewels coming out of your mouth! What kind of witchcraft is this?"

Then Hyacinth remembered the old woman's words. The strange promise had come true! It took a long time to explain everything to her mother, because as she spoke, rubies, emeralds, lilies and violets rolled off her tongue. When her story was done, a small fortune lay on the ground at her feet.

Her mother was astonished. She was also greedy. She ran to Rose. She could double her fortune.

"Look what your sister got just for giving an old hag a drop of water! Go to the fountain, Rose. When the old woman comes again and asks you for a drink of water, offer it to her nicely."

promise, the old woman vanished.

Hyacinth smiled and shook her head. What a strange old woman! She picked up the heavy jug and hurried home, not giving the old woman another thought.

Hyacinth could hear her mother yelling before she even stepped into the house. "Where have you been, you lazy thing!? You haven't made the beds! You haven't fed the hens! And your sister and I have been waiting for lunch!"

"I'm sorry, Mother," Hyacinth began, "but when I went to get water ..." she stopped. Two roses, a pearl, and a diamond had fallen from her mouth. The widow's eyes widened.

"What on earth is happen-

mother refused to spend the money to have a well dug near the house. So, twice a day, Hyacinth had to go to the spring well which was in a dark area, deep in the forest. She was always a little frightened when she went.

One day, while she was filling her heavy water jug at the spring, Hyacinth saw someone approaching through the trees. It was a ragged, old woman, leaning on a stick. Her face was kind and gentle.

"Could you get me a drop of water, dear child?" the old woman asked. "I've been walking for so long, and I'm tired, and thirsty."

"Why, of course!" Hyacinth carefully rinsed out the jug and filled it with fresh cool water before she offered it to the old woman.

When she had drunk her fill, the old woman said, "You're not just beautiful; you are generous and good as well. I would like to give you a gift. From now on, whenever you speak, flowers and jewels will spring from your lips."

As soon as she made the

Rose and the widow lived in comfort but were not content. They yelled out a steady stream of orders for poor Hyacinth to do.

"Hyacinth, collect the eggs immediately."

"Hyacinth, clean the hearth until it sparkles."

"Hyacinth, iron my petticoats right away."

Hyacinth always did as she was told.

Her mother and sister feasted at the dining room table, stuffing themselves with delicious meals, wine, and tasty sweets. Hyacinth, however, ate cold leftovers in the kitchen. She had to be ready to answer their call in an instant.

Although she was a wonderful cook, they refused to praise her. "The chicken is burnt!" they said. "The cake hasn't risen enough," they whined. "The coffee is too hot," they complained, or, "The coffee is too cold."

Poor Hyacinth! What a terrible life she led! Other young girls nearby met in the village square. They had fun together, gossipping, visiting, playing games. They went to parties and wore pretty clothes. A few of them even had boyfriends. Hyacinth was never part of the goings-on.

After her father's death, Hyacinth almost never left the house, except to take care of some chore. She saw no one except her mother and sister. She never had a moment to herself and she did not know that she grew more beautiful every day.

Despite the hard work and loneliness, Hyacinth remained kind and gentle. She took care of all her tasks cheerfully and without complaint.

The most difficult of all her chores was getting water. Her

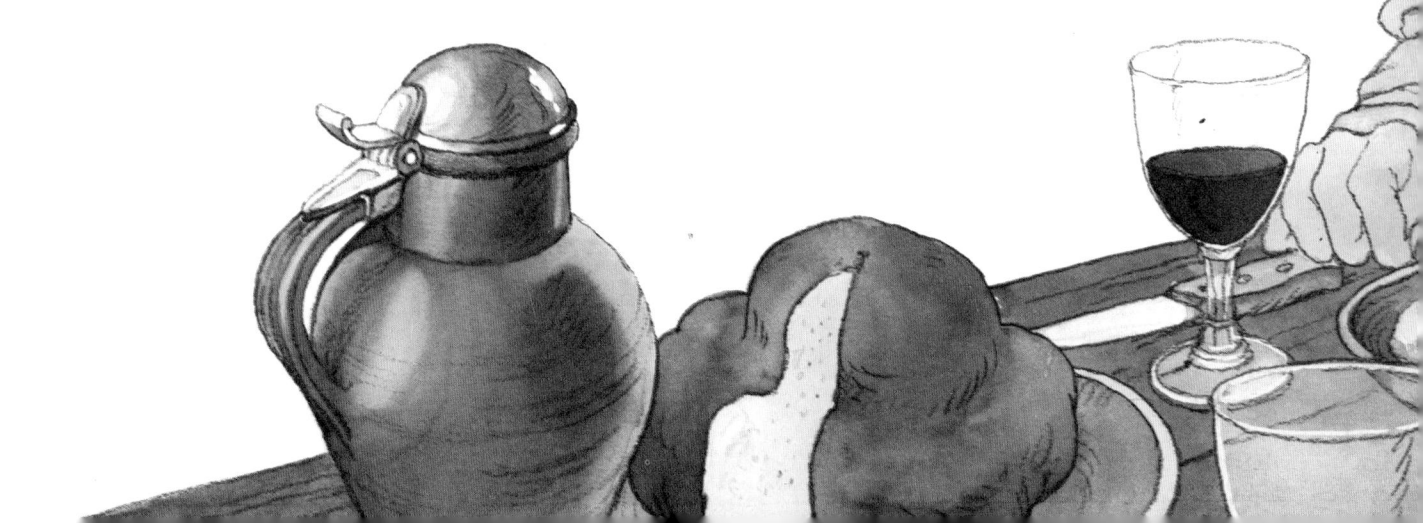

TOADS AND DIAMONDS

Once upon a time there was a widow with two daughters, Hyacinth and Rose. Rose was older and just like her mother. That is, she was ugly, rude, and greedy. Naturally, she was her mother's favorite.

Hyacinth, on the other hand, took after her late father. She was beautiful, kind, and good-hearted, always willing to help others. Her mother and sister hated her. They treated her worse than they would a servant.

They demanded that Hyacinth take care of all the heavy chores which they didn't want to do. She had to collect firewood, look after the hens, get water from the spring and do all the housework.